P9-CZV-871
Withdrawn

POTATOES ON TUESDAY

By Dee Lillegard
Illustrated by David McPhail

GoodYearBooks

On Monday, cabbage,

On Tuesday, potatoes,

On Wednesday, carrots,

On Thursday, tomatoes.

On Friday, peas and
green beans, too—

On Saturday, a great big pot of . . .

stew!
Mmmm.